To..
....
....
This book invites you
to a Halloween Scare

D0717820

Prepare If You Dare

A Halloween Scare at MY HOUSE

To my own little monster, Max, and his marvellous mum x

Visit the author's website! http://ericjames.co.uk

Written by Eric James
Illustrated by Marina Le Ray, Amerigo Pinelli
and Natalie & Tamsin Hinrichsen
Designed by Sarah Allen

First published by HOMETOWN WORLD in 2014
Hometown World Ltd
7 Northumberland Buildings
Bath BA1 2JB

www.hometownworld.co.uk

ISBN 978-1-84993-780-1
All rights reserved
Printed in China

10 9 8 7 6 5 4 3 2

Prepare If You Dare

A Halloween Scare at MY HOUSE

Written by Eric James

Illustrated by Marina Le Ray

CHILDHOOD DREAMS
HOMETOWN WORLD

Prepare, if you dare,
for a **terrible scare**,
A night of pure terror to whiten your hair,

A tale full of sights that are best left unseen.
'You ready? 'You sure?
This was my Halloween...

The werewolves
ho**wled loudly**.
The moon shone so bright.
I stayed in my bedroom,
the curtains shut tight.

My heart started pounding,
my knees felt so weak,
But, being a brave kid,
I just **had** to peek.

I pulled back the curtains. My mouth opened wide.
An army of monsters had gathered outside!
They staggered and stumbled and lurched down the streets
With bags full of lollipops, chocolates and sweets.

Emerging from sewers and alleys and drains
Came creatures and critters with cravings for brains.
And more came to join them from places nearby,
On buses, on broomsticks, by road and by sky.

From **north** and from **south**, **from** the **west** and the **east**,
From every direction came all Kinds of beast.

They gathered together
for one **spooky** night,
To seek out the living
and give them a **fright**.

The thunder clapped loudly with terrible booms.
The witches dodged lightning and clung to their brooms.
The two-headed doggies tried chasing their tails,
And banshees let loose with their hideous wails.

The vampires hung out
on the street in their gangs,
And grinned, just to show off
their pearly white fangs.

JUST MARRIED

The mummies moaned loudly and swayed side to side,
While Frankenstein stomped about town with his bride.

A crazy inventor
was harnessing lightning,
And up in his lab he did
something quite frightening.

He made his own monster,
half dog and half shark.
I heard that its bite
was much worse than its bark!

A silly old wizard,
with very bad sight,
Bumped into another
(which started a fight!).

A hapless young local
who stood in the road
Was struck by a spell
and turned into a toad!

The creepies were crawly, the crazies were crazed,
The shuffling zombies had eyes that were glazed.
The **gigantic** ogres were as ugly as sin,
With big bulging noses and warts on their chin.

The ghouls danced around but were lacking in soul,
The gargoyles could rock, and the headless could roll!
Although the whole spectacle seemed to spell doom,
I foolishly thought I'd be safe in my room!

But then something happened
that made my heart jump.
From somewhere below me
I heard a big THUMP!

THE QUEEN

I froze for a moment, as quiet as a mouse.

Yes, I could hear noises from INSIDE THE HOUSE!

I put on my slippers

and pulled on my robe.

I shook like a leaf

but I don't think it showed.

Then, slowly but surely,

I crept down the stairs,

Preparing myself for the
biggest of scares.

My hands trembled wildly.
I opened the door.
I still shudder now
at the horrors I saw.
The stereo spat out
some hideous sounds
As dozens of monsters
jumped madly around.

The sight was horrific. It made my skin crawl.
These monsters were having their
Halloween Ball!

And right in the middle, one monster loomed tall,
The hairiest, scariest monster of all...

He turned round and saw me.
I fell to my knees.
"I'm not very tasty,
so don't eat me, please!"

He beamed ear-to-ear
and broke free from the huddle,

Ran over,
and gave me a...

BIG

MONSTER

CUDDLE!

"At last!
We have found you!" he said with a smile.
"We've roamed everywhere and
we've looked for a while.

BEST COSTUME

"We came here to give you your wonderful prize."
He held up a trophy in front of my eyes.

"A prize? And for me?"

I replied with a grin.
"But what did I enter and how did I win?"
"You've won the first prize for the costume you're wearing!
It even scares me, and I'm old-hat at scaring!"

"This isn't a costume. I'm just dressed as me!"

"Exactly, the scariest thing you can be!

A small human child, with a cute button nose.

Your teeth are so shiny, you've only ten toes.

No hair on your face and no horns on your head.

The whites of your eyes are not glowing or red!

A bone-chilling costume! A horrible sight!

A worthy ensemble
for Halloween night!"

We partied together
until the moon set,
A Halloween night
that I'll never forget.

And next year I won't
want to hide in my bed.
The monsters won't scare me...